the
NECROPHILIAC

the NECROPHILIAC

(NÉCROPHILE)

le

GABRIELLE WITTKOP

Translated from the French by

DON BAPST

MISFIT

ECW Press

Published by ECW Press
665 Gerrard Street East, Toronto, Ontario, Canada M4M 1Y2
416.694.3348 / info@ecwpress.com

LIBRARY AND ARCHIVES CANADA CATALOGUING IN PUBLICATION

Wittkop, Gabrielle, 1920–2002
The necrophiliac / Gabrielle Wittkop ; translated by Don Bapst.

Translation of: Le nécrophile.
ISBN 978-1-55022-943-1

I. Bapst, Don II. Title.

PQ2683.I82N413 2011   843'.914   C2010-906687-I

Developing editor: Michael Holmes / a misFit book
Cover and Text Design: Tania Craan
Typesetting: Rachel Ironstone
Production: Troy Cunningham
6

This book has been supported by the French Ministry of Foreign and European
Affairs, as part of the translation grant program.

PRINTED AND BOUND IN CANADA

To the memory of C.D.,
who fell into death like Narcissus into his own image.

October 12, 19...

The grey eyelashes of this little girl cast a grey shadow against her cheek. She has the sly, ironic smile of those who know a lot. Two uncurled locks frame her face, descending to the hem of her blouse, which has been pulled up under her armpits to reveal a stomach of the same bluish white seen in certain Chinese porcelain. The mound of Venus, very flat, very smooth, shines slightly in the lamplight; it seems to be covered in a film of sweat.

I spread the thighs to study the vulva, thin as a scar, the transparent lips a pale mauve. But I still have to wait a few hours; for the moment, the whole body is still a bit stiff, a bit clenched, until the heat of the room softens it like wax. This little girl is worth the trouble. It's truly a very beautiful dead girl.

October 13, 19...

Yesterday evening, the little girl played a mean trick on me. I should have been more careful of her with that smile of hers. While I was sliding

✳

into that flesh so cold, so soft, so deliciously
tight, found only in the dead, the child abruptly
opened an eye, translucent like that of an
octopus, and with a terrifying gurgling, she
threw up a black stream of mysterious liquid on
me. Open in a Gorgon mask, her mouth didn't
stop vomiting this juice until its odour filled
the room. All this rather spoiled my pleasure.
I'm accustomed to better manners, for the dead
are tidy. They have already released their
excrement in leaving life as one disposes of an
ignominious burden. Also, their bellies
resound with the hard, hollow sound of drums.
Their fine powerful odour is that of the bombyx.
It seems to come from the heart of the earth,
from the empire where the musky larvae trudge
between the roots, where blades of mica gleam
like frozen silver, there where the blood of
future chrysanthemums wells up, among the
dusty peat, the sulphureous mire. The smell of
the dead is that of the return to the cosmos, that
of the sublime alchemy. For nothing is as flawless
as a corpse, and it becomes more and more so as

✳

time passes, until the final purity of this large ivory doll with its mute smile and its perpetually spread legs that is in each one of us.

I had to spend more than two hours cleaning the bed and washing the little girl. This child, who vomits such putrid ink, truly has the nature of the octopus. For the moment she seems to have disgorged all of her venoms, spread out wisely over the sheets. Her false smile. Her little hands with the little nails. A blue fly that came from I don't know where constantly lands and lands again on her thigh. This little girl quickly stopped pleasing me. She's not one of the dead from whom I have any grief in separating myself, the way one deplores having to leave a friend. She certainly had a mean character, I would swear to it. From time to time, she emits a deep gurgling that makes me suspicious.

October 14, 19...

Tonight, while I was getting ready to wrap the little girl in a plastic bag so I could throw her in the Seine near Sèvres, as I am used to doing in such a case, she suddenly emitted a desperate sigh. Pained, prolonged, the S in Sèvres whistled between her teeth as if she had already suffered some sort of intolerable sorrow over her next abandonment. An immense pity squeezed at my heart. I hadn't done justice to the humble, harsh charm of this child. I threw myself on her, covered her with kisses, repentant as an unfaithful lover. I went to look for a brush in the bathroom and began styling her hair, which had become flat and broken; I rubbed her body with oils, perfumes. And I don't know how many times I loved that child, until day lightened the window behind the closed curtains.

October 15, 19...

The road for Sèvres is the road for all flesh, and the sighs of the vomiting girl won't do anything about it. Alas!

November 2, 19...

Festival of the dead. Lucky day. Montparnasse Cemetery was admirably grey this morning. The immense crowd of mourners squeezed into its walkways among the glorious chrysanthemums, and the air had the bitter, intoxicating taste of love. Eros and Thanatos. All these sexes under the earth, does anyone ever think of them?

The night falls quickly. Even though it's the festival of the dead, I won't go out tonight.

I remember. I'd just turned eight. One night in November, similar to this one today, I was left alone in my room, which was invaded by shadow. I was worried that the house was full of strange comings and goings, full of mysterious whispers that, I felt, had something to do with my mother's illness. Above all, I felt she had forgotten me. I don't know why I didn't dare to turn on the lights, lying silent and afraid in the dark. I was getting bored. To distract and console myself, I tried unbuttoning my little trousers. There I found that sweet, hot little thing that always kept me company. I no longer know how my hand discovered the necessary movements, but I was suddenly captured in a vortex of pleasures from which it seemed nothing in the world could ever free me. I surprised myself beyond the limits of imagination to discover such a resource for pleasure in my very own flesh and to feel my proportions modify themselves in a way that I didn't even suspect just moments before. I sped up my movements and my pleasure grew but, at the very moment that a wave — born in the depths of my entrails — seemed to want to submerge me and lift me above myself, quick steps resounded in the corridor, the door opened abruptly, the light flashed in. Pale, haggard, my grandmother held herself at the threshold and her trouble was so great that she didn't even notice the state I was in. "My poor child! Your mother is dead." Then, grabbing me by the hand, she forcefully dragged me with her. I was wearing a sailor suit, and thankfully the coat was long enough to mask the fly that I hadn't had the time to close.

My mother's room was full of people, but sunken in a half-darkness. I noticed my father on his knees at the bedside, and he was crying, his head stuffed into the sheets. At first I had trouble recognizing my mother in this woman who seemed infinitely more beautiful, grand, young, and majestic than she had ever seemed until then. Grandmother was sobbing. "Kiss your mother again once more," she said, pushing me towards the bed. I brought myself up to this marvellous woman stretched out among the whiteness of the linen. I placed my lips on her waxen face; I squeezed her shoulders in my little arms; I breathed in her intoxicating odour. It was that of the bombyx that the natural history professor had passed out at school and that I had brought up in a cardboard box. That fine, dry, musky odour of leaves, larvae, and stones was leaving Mother's lips; it was already seeping out into her hair like a perfume. And suddenly, the interrupted pleasure took over my childish flesh with a disconcerting abruptness. Pressed against Mother's shoulder, I felt a delicious commotion rush over me while I poured my heart out for the first time.

"Poor child!" said Grandmother, who had understood nothing about my sighs.

✳

People always say that those who love the dead are stricken with anosmia. For me, there's nothing to that, and my nose perceives the most diverse odours vividly, even if, like everyone, I am accustomed to those of my surroundings to the point of no longer being able to smell them. It could, in fact, be possible that the odour of bombyx impregnates my whole apartment without my even noticing.

The ladies show no signs of having any special trouble cleaning the antique store I inherited from my father. At the very most, once in a while, there's a vague grumbling over the old objects, the nests of dust, the fragile things that are so ugly even though new ones could be purchased for much less. It's only in my private apartment, on the fifth floor, that their behavior causes me to reflect. They stare into the corners with a look of prudent suspicion. They observe me slyly, and, most of all, they sniff the apartment's odour, shifting their eyes. They sniff and sniff, searching their memory, finding nothing that's

right; sniff again, until a strange worry spreads
over them. Then they become hunted beasts
and escape. When I try to get them back to work,
they give me the most vague answers with a
frightened look, shaking their heads if I offer to
increase their wages. I put a new ad into the
papers and the same story begins again. One
day, however, one of the cleaning ladies had the
courage to ask me why I always wore black clothes,
even though I wasn't in mourning. Another,
very young, already fat, and whose name I've
forgotten, declared in a local store that I smelled
like a vampire. Always this old and aberrant
confusion between two beings so fundamentally
opposed as the vampire and the necrophiliac,
between the dead that feed off the living and
the living who love the dead. I don't deny,
nevertheless, that after several days, the perfume
of the bombyx transforms itself into an odour
like that of heated metal that, more and more
acrid, thickens finally into a stench of entrails.
Each of these stages has its charm — even if the
last announces separation — but never would I

✳

have the idea to eat the flesh of one of my
friends, the dead, nor to drink the blood.

As for the concierge, for a long while now she
has stopped being surprised that I don't have a
"girlfriend." And since the slightest "boyfriend"
has never appeared either, she simply concluded
that I am a sort of Joseph, a real loner. All the
better. There are certain truths that rudimentary
souls would have trouble accepting. My
boyfriends with anuses glacial as mint, my
exquisite mistresses with grey marble bellies, I
bring them at night into my old Chevrolet, while
everyone sleeps, and I take them all back to the
bridge at Sèvres or the one at Asnières.

December 3, 19…

This morning, while I was taking care of my
correspondence, a client made a request that
troubled me. It was a man of around forty years,
with a ruddy complexion in the first stages of
baldness, dressed like a lawyer or the director
of a business. He looked over the furniture, the
porcelain, the paintings, but mostly the curios,

✳

seemingly looking for something. Then finally,
approaching my table: "Tell me, sir, don't you
have any amusing netsuke? It's specifically those
of Koshi Muramato that I'm thinking of." For
a second, our stares met. How many know Koshi
Muramato, the master of the eighteenth century,
who, in his Kyushu workshop, consecrated
himself exclusively to macabre netsuke? The
dead sodomized by hyenas, fellating succubi,
masturbating skeletons, cadavers interlaced like
nests of vipers, fetus-devouring phantoms,
courtesans impaling themselves on the stiffness
of a dead body. . . .

"I'm sorry," I responded, "but usually the
people who own the works of this master hesitate
to give them up. Nevertheless, if you would like
to leave me your address, I can, if I happen to
find something . . ."

He refused with a curtness that made me
suspect that he had understood I would never
sell him anything of this sort. The netsuke of
Koshi Muramato — I save them for myself! Only

✳

a necrophiliac can collect these objects, and the man intrigued me.

"Would your prefer to stop in again?" I suggested.

"I don't live in Paris. It's very rare that I come here."

He nodded goodbye and left. I wouldn't have disliked discussing the macabre netsuke with him: offer him a few words — certainly vain — then smile at him knowingly. Not to offer him fuller knowledge, but to see if he would grasp that I understood. That's all. For if necrophiliacs — they are so rare — recognize each other, they don't look for each other. They have definitely chosen incommunicability, and their loves transcend into the inexpressible. Alone, we are not even the link between life and death. There is no link. For life and death are forever united, inseparable as water mixed with wine.

I cannot prevent myself from laughing as — without missing a beat — I remove from my vest pocket a netsuke that I carry with me constantly. It measures no more than three centimetres and represents two peasants fucking the sockets of a skull with great skill.

December 4, 19...

The visit from the netsuke lover brought back to mind those few unusual meetings in which necrophilia revealed itself in others. Frankly, nothing very sensational or frequent. I remember, for example, a funeral I attended when I was about twenty. I found myself there that time not out of taste, but convenience; it was a distant relative whose disagreeable appearance and repulsive disposition removed any desire to visit his coffin. It was during the absolution; the priest was chanting; some women were sobbing. In the private chapel, the air was scarce, and the catafalque took up almost all the central space — the perfume of flowers, candles, and incense revealed itself with the subtle hint of bombyx. I soon noticed that I wasn't the only one to notice it. I found myself in one of the miniscule aisles where the shadows were very thick, though not quite thick enough

❋

to prevent me from making out an extremely banal couple dressed in mourning, whom I guessed — I don't know why — had come to enjoy themselves. No doubt the music, the funereal chants, and the bombyx had the custom of acting on the man in a specific way, for I distinctly heard his companion whisper to him a precise question on the state he found himself in. She used a vulgar word, something from an army barracks, of a crudeness that took me aback. There was, I believe, another outline of a gesture, but I wasn't sure. Either he was too timid to advance any further or he preferred the intimacy of his room, but the couple made haste to leave the chapel. The black clothes of the woman brushed against me as she passed. She had the milky, fixed stare of a blind woman.

These two were only watered-down necrophiliacs, and their preferences couldn't rise to the height of passion. But there are others that hesitate at nothing, and I remember a bad encounter at Montmartre Cemetery only last year.

An actress I knew as a client had just been interred — a woman neither beautiful nor ugly, insignificant enough to seem to never be able to inspire extreme emotions. As soon as I knew she was dead, I wanted her terribly. I arrived at the cemetery in a torrential rain that certainly wasn't going to facilitate my task. I picked the lock on the gardener's tool shed, as I am accustomed to do, in order to procure a spade. I always operate with great speed and it never takes me more than an hour to open the grave, descend into it, raise the coffin lid with a cold chisel, and, weighed down with the body, climb back to the surface using a carefully perfected technique. There remains nothing left to do but transport it to my car, the only consistent difficulty being the hoisting of the body over the wall with the help of a rope.

That night, the horrible rain slowed down my movements; engorged with water, the earth was heavy. What's more, the meteorologists had predicted that the precipitation would last fifteen days and I couldn't wait that long. As I struggled

✳

to climb out of the slippery grave with my
package, I saw a man who was hiding behind a
tombstone to watch me. His dark silhouette, his
thick neck detached themselves neatly from the
depth of the night. An atrocious fear spread
over me. This man was going to follow me, kill
me maybe. Or more likely, he was going to
denounce me. Without knowing what I was
doing, I abandoned the actress and fled as fast
as my anguish permitted me. I cleared the wall
in a single bound, and it wasn't until I had
arrived at home that, little by little, I regained
my composure. I was certain I hadn't been
followed. That man had nothing against me.

The next day, in reading the paper I obtained
an abominable surprise. In Montmartre
Cemetery, the body of a well-known actress
had been discovered, stripped of its clothes,
disemboweled and horribly mutilated. The rain
had effaced all clues. So the revolting man who
had spied on me had taken advantage of the
fruit of my efforts. How horrible! I burst into
tears of vexation and grief.

December 22, 19...

I went this morning for a stroll around the Ivry
Cemetery, charming under the snow like an
ornate centrepiece made of sugar, strangely lost
in a plebeian district. Watching a widow decorate
the tomb of the deceased with a little Christmas
tree, I noticed suddenly how rare they've
become, those women in full mourning in
their floating veils — though often blond — who
haunted necropolises twenty years ago. It was,
for the most part — usually, not always —
professionals who practised their art behind
the family monuments with an absolutely
depressing absence of brilliance and sincerity.
Widows' meat.

January 1, 19...

I celebrate the New Year in good company, that
of a concierge from rue de Vaugirard, dead of
an embolism. (I often learn of this sort of
detail during the course of a burial.) This little
old woman is certainly no beauty, but she is
extremely pleasant, light to carry, silent and

23

supple, agreeable despite her eyes that have
fallen back into her head like those of a doll.
Her dentures have been removed, which causes
her cheeks to sink in, but when I strip off her
awful nylon blouse, she surprises me with the
breasts of a young woman: firm, silky, absolutely
intact — her New Year's gift.

With her, love is imprinted with a certain
calm. She doesn't inflame my flesh; she refreshes
it. Normally so miserly with the time I spend
with the dead — time that runs away very quickly
— trying to take advantage of each second in their
company, I lay next to her last night to sleep a
few hours like a husband next to his spouse, an
arm slipped under the thin neck, a hand resting
on the belly where I had found a certain joy.

The little concierge's name is Marie-Jeanne
Chaulard, a name that the Goncourt brothers
would certainly have appreciated.

The breasts are truly remarkable. In pushing
them together, a tight passage is obtained, plump,
infinitely soft.

I lightly caress the hair — thin, grey, pulled

back — the neck and shoulders where a silver slime, like that left by snails, is drying now. . . .

January 11, 19...

My tailor — a tailor who maintains the devoted manners of a bygone era and who speaks to me in the third person — finally couldn't prevent himself from suggesting a less morose wardrobe for me. "For however elegant, black is sad." And so it's the colour that suits me, for I am also sad. I am sad that today I must separate from those I love. The tailor smiles at me in the mirror. This man believes he understands my body because he knows how I dress the manhood in my pants and because he discovered with surprise that the muscles of my arms are abnormally developed for a man of my profession. If he knew what purpose these fine muscles could also serve. . . . If he knew what use I have for this manhood, which he once noted in his book that I wear to the left. . . .

Gabrielle Wittkop

✳

A client this morning had a few nice words for an eighteenth century Portuguese mariners' chest. "How beautiful it is! You'd think it was a coffin!" What's more, she bought it.

May 12, 19...

I can't see a pretty woman or a handsome man without immediately wishing he or she were dead. Once, back in the days of my adolescence, I actually wished it with passion and fury. There was a neighbour three or four years older than me, a tall brunette girl with green eyes I saw almost every day. Even though I wanted to, it never would have occurred to me to merely touch her hand. I waited; I wanted her death and that death became for me the pole around which all my thoughts gravitated. *Shall I then say that I longed with an earnest and consuming desire for the moment of Morella's decease? I did.* More than once, the mere meeting of that young girl — her name was Gabrielle — threw me into a tremendous excitement that I knew, however, would pass the

very instant that I took it upon myself to make
the first move. Instead, I spent hours picturing
all the dangers and ways of death that could
strike down Gabrielle. I loved to represent
myself on her deathbed, imagining the exact
details of the environment: the flowers, the
candles, the funereal odour, the paling lips and
the badly shut lids revealing the whites of the
eyes. One time, meeting her by chance in the
stairs, I noticed that my neighbour had a painful
cut at the corner of her mouth. I was young, in
love, and romantic, which led me to
immediately conclude that she had a secret
penchant for suicide. I ran and locked myself in
my room, threw myself on the bed, and devoted
myself to solitary pleasures. In my mind's eye, I
saw Gabrielle delicately balanced, hanged from a
ceiling hook. From time to time, the body,
dressed in a white lace slip, turned at the end of
the rope, offering a look at every possible angle.
The face pleased me greatly, even though it was
inclined and half-concealed by the hair, sinking
that enormous tongue — which was almost black

and filled the open mouth like a spray of vomit — into shadow. The arms — a beautiful dull brown — hung from gently dislocated shoulders; the shoeless feet were pointed inward.

I renewed this fantasy without modifying anything every time my desire demanded it, and for a long time it brought me intense pleasure. But Gabrielle left town; not seeing her anymore, I ended up forgetting her, and the image that had caused me so much joy was eventually worn out in its own time.

August 3, 19...

Henri, dead of scarlet fever at six — though I never catch the slightest sickness — is a brave little man. He has the perfect body for playing with, for enjoying, even though games and pleasures have to take place on the external surfaces. This child is so tight that I have to renounce more profound delights at the risk of hurting both of us. In vain I tried various techniques, some of which I was naive enough to think infallible. But Henri is succulent the way

he is. The inside of his thighs, slightly concave,
allow for an almost perfect union. As he is,
unfortunately, quite advanced already, I don't
know if I will be able to keep this child much
longer. Besides, I'm hardly saving him, not
hesitating to play with him in warm baths despite
the fact that I know, unfortunately, they advance
his degradation. His flesh softens from hour to
hour; his greening stomach sinks in, rumbling
with bad flatulence that bursts into enormous
bubbles in the bathwater. Even worse: his face
frowns and becomes alien to him; I don't
recognize my little Henri anymore.

August 7, 19...

Yesterday evening, I took my leave from Henri
whose odour was becoming intolerable. I had
prepared a strongly perfumed bath so that I
could once more press the deliquescent little
body against mine. Henri gave me a surprise,
for the dead are full of the unexpected — I think
of Marie-Jeanne's breasts; I think of still others.
He finally permitted me to really penetrate his

flesh, softened as a melting wax: his way of sweetening our farewell. I dried him in a bath towel; I put back the little blue brushed cotton pajamas he was wearing when he arrived; I smoothed out his brown bangs that the bathwater made to seem almost black. In the car, I had seated him next to me, supporting him with one hand, driving with the other. I drove slowly; I was not in a hurry to arrive. As always in such cases, I had a heavy heart. "No, not yet," I repeated. I crossed the Seine at Saint-Cloud, but it was only at Maisons-Laffitte that I had the necessary courage. I returned to Paris in a long procession of trucks and tractors, the smell of crushed grass, the blasts from car horns, the gleam of headlights. Suddenly, I saw my face in the rearview mirror inundated with tears.

November 20, 19...

I won't go out tonight. I don't want to see anyone and I would like to have the store completely closed by the afternoon. Four years ago to the day, I had to take leave of Suzanne.

At that time, I wasn't yet keeping a journal, but, now, I want to write to relive the story of my meeting with Suzanne.

It all started in a dramatic, dangerous fashion, and right from the start we were threatened together, the one by the other, the one for the other. It was an autumn evening, very warm, a bit foggy, the sidewalks glistening with wet leaves. November always brings me something unexpected even if it has always been prepared. I went to look for Suzanne in the Montparnasse Cemetery. Waiting. Anticipated happiness, like every time. I only knew her name, that she was thirty-six, that she was married, without a career. Very strange to know her. Everything went normally and I had no trouble hoisting her over the wall; she was little and thin. I guessed I had no more than a dozen steps along boulevard Edgar-Quinet before I reached rue Huyghens, where I had left my car, but the fog had probably misled me, for I very quickly found myself out of the cemetery and well short of the place I had envisioned. I hurried as best I could, glad that

Suzanne was so light, when I suddenly thought my heart was going to stop. Two cops on patrol were coming to meet me. They weren't hurrying, but they blocked the only possible retreat; already I could distinctly hear the atrocious squeal of tires. Holding Suzanne firmly in my arms, I threw her against the cemetery wall. Happily, she wasn't dressed in one of those horrible funeral gowns but wore an ordinary jersey suit and street shoes. Out of the terrifying squeal of tires, a headlight beam touched our legs: those belonging to a kissing couple. Behind me, the hostile world, cops, stupidity, hatred. In front of me, this unknown woman, her face tilted in the shadow of my own, this woman who was called Suzanne and for the love of whom I was risking my own destruction. I thought the moment would never end, until a voice already en route towards Raspail barked, "Oh shit, nice lovers' spot . . ."

It took me I don't know how many centuries to overcome the paralysis into which the terror rooted me — immobilized as in a nightmare — and start walking again to my car. Even though

I wasn't stupid enough to measure the value of things by the difficulties involved in conquering them, I already knew that this trial was the counterpart of unspeakable bliss.

Suzanne . . . A petty bourgeois with finely coiffed blond hair, a polka-dot blouse under a classic suit. Her wedding ring had been removed. At this hour, her husband wore it, broken down with grief — or maybe not — between the green plants, the sideboard, and the television set, somewhere in the apartment on the rue de Sèvres.

Rue de Sèvres . . . The Sèvres bridge . . .

She wasn't pretty, probably never even was, just nice with her turned-up nose, her eyebrows raised in great surprise. Now death must have surprised her, maybe between the items purchased from the supermarket and the apple tart confection, mowed down in one swift blow, by a heart attack or something like that. There was no sign of a fight or even an appeasement, nothing. Nothing of the surprise of being dead. Suzanne had soft skin, almond-shaped nails. In

※

lifting her blouse, I noticed the carefully shaved armpits. She was wearing underwear made of a crêpe de Chine of a quality far superior to that of her suit, from which I concluded a dignity, a genuine feminine modesty. Her body showed that she had always respected it with a sort of asceticism, but a likeable, civilized, lenient asceticism.

Suzanne . . . The Lily . . . There is purity each time that a new threshold is crossed. She had crossed that of death.

I sensed from the first moment what Suzanne would be for me. Also, even if very chilly, I lost no time in turning off the heat, establishing those sly drafts that refrigerate the rooms in a moment and last for hours. I prepared some ice. I kept Suzanne away from everything that could harm her. Except me, alas!

I returned to her, impatient as a young spouse. Her delicious odour of bombyx was just as it should be. I carried Suzanne to my bed. With a trembling hand, I removed her bra, her little panties. The wait took away my trembling;

the tension of my desire didn't permit me to
prolong the moment of possession any further.
I threw myself on that charming dead girl, and
without even removing her garters or her
stockings, I took her with a fury and violence
that I don't believe I had ever experienced.

In the morning, I went down to the
concierge, begging her not to disturb me for any
reason. I pretended I had some urgent and
difficult work to do, the restoration of a very
precious painting, a task that I had never before
executed. She seemed to half believe me despite
the strange glance she shot me.

I locked myself in with Suzanne. Honeymoon
without music and without bouquets in my glacial
room where the lamps burned. I didn't respond
to the telephone. One or two times, despite my
forbidding, someone rang the doorbell. My
heart beating, holding my breath, immobile in
the dark vestibule, I was all ready to do anything
to defend my treasure.

I surrounded Suzanne with bags of ice. I
often applied cologne to her face, which was

marvellously intact, except for that greyish gleam
that attaches itself to the cheekbones and that
delicate pinching that refines the nose of the
dead. Three days after her arrival, Suzanne
opened her mouth suddenly, as if to say
something. She had beautifully formed teeth.
Didn't I say that the dead always have surprises
to share? They are so good, the dead. . . .

For fourteen days, I was unspeakably happy.
Unspeakably but not absolutely because, for me,
joy never comes without the grief of knowing it
is only ephemeral. All happiness carries with it
the seed of its own end. Only death, mine, will
deliver me from defeat, from the wound that
time inflicts on us. With Suzanne, I experienced
all the pleasures without exhausting them. I
covered her with caresses. I tenderly licked her
sex; I grabbed her greedily; I plunged myself
into her again and again without stop, for at the
time I didn't have a preference for the delights
of Sodom. Then Suzanne let out a light
whistling that could have been described as
admiring or politely ironic, a breath that

✳

seemed to not want to finish, a sweet, prolonged complaint: Sssss . . . S as in Sèvres . . .

Suzanne, my beautiful Lily, the joy of my soul and of my flesh, had started to marbleise with violet patches. I multiplied the bags of ice. I had wanted to keep Suzanne forever. I kept her for almost two weeks, barely sleeping, feeding myself with what I found in the fridge, drinking too much at times. The tick-tock of the pendulums, the creaking of the woodwork had adopted a particular quality, just like each time Death is present. She is the great mathematician who gives the exact value to the data in a problem.

As time passed and the dust deposited an ashy veil over everything, my despair over having to leave Suzanne grew. The craziest ideas entered my mind. The primary one, though, never left me. I told myself I should have taken Suzanne abroad — but where? — right on that first night, before having even made her my mistress. I should have had her embalmed and I would never have had to separate myself from her. That would have been happiness. Instead, I had

gone crazy, crazy and bad; I never had the
wisdom to overcome and defer my desire; I had
lost, out of the coarseness of my sex, a body that
could have always delighted my senses and my
heart. Now it was too late, I could no longer
have Suzanne embalmed. Regret and pain
gripped me in a terrible stranglehold. But
hardly had I said it was too late and that I had
wasted everything, when I rushed out again to
the foot of my mistress, covering her legs with
kisses where already the shaven down was starting
to grow again. Desire seized me again with more
force than grief, and soon I found myself
interlaced with Suzanne, my mouth on her
mouth, my belly on hers.

Passion and grief had invaded me to such a
point that I didn't bathe or shave anymore, and
mirrors reflected back the image of a shaggy,
livid man with sunken eyes bordered in red.
Seated at Suzanne's bedside, a bottle near me,
enveloped in woolen blankets to ward off the
cold, I imagined finding myself in my own
tomb. Sounds from the outside barely reached

✳

me, almost never crossing the drawn curtains anymore: the clear sound of garbage cans pulled at dawn along the sidewalk.

The last night, I washed Suzanne; I put back on her fine underwear, her bourgeois suit that two weeks earlier I had removed euphorically. Wrapped in a rug, I carried her to the car. Green Suzanne, blue Suzanne, already inhabited, I think. The moment I let her slip into the Seine, I let out a cry that I heard resonate as if it had come from another planet. It seemed someone had ripped out my heart, ripped off my sex.

The Seine had welcomed her body, which had been saturated by my sweat and engorged by my semen for two weeks. My life, my death, mixed in Suzanne. In her, I entered into Hades; with her, I travelled all the way into the oceanic silt, tangled myself in the seaweed, petrified myself into the limestone, circulated into the veins of coral. . . .

Back at home, I threw myself on a bed that smelled of decay. I fell asleep instantly, brutally seized by a mortal slumber, rocked to sleep by

the same black waves — *mare tenebrarum* — that
rocked Suzanne, Suzanne my love.

December 1, 19...

I don't hate my occupation: its cadaverous
ivories, its pallid crockery, all the goods of the
dead, the furniture that they made, the tables
that they painted, the glasses from which they
drank when life was still sweet to them. Truly,
the occupation of an antiquarian is a situation
almost ideal for a necrophiliac.

December 30, 19...

At my neighbour's house, in the library, an
elegant stamp from the eighteenth century — a
nun toiling for a monk — that reminded me of a
burlesque episode that occurred a dozen years ago.

I had gone to Melun on business that I
managed to complete in much less time than
I'd expected. Having arrived by train, I still had
more than two full hours to kill. Now, I knew
that a *Circumcision*, by Gentile Bellini, was located
in the chapel des Filles in Saint-Thomas-de-

Villeneuve, right in the north gallery. As these
nuns aren't cloistered, their chapel is open to
the public. The owner of the restaurant where I
had lunched told me some pretty horrible things
about the notorious hysteria and meanness of
these nuns towards the orphans they took in.
The convent was situated at the edge of the city.

It was suffocatingly hot and stormy, and
everyone seemed to be sleeping. The garden
gate was wide open, as was the chapel door where
I entered without being seen. The stairs to the
galleries were immediately to the right, and I
followed them right away. I found the *Circumcision*,
which disappointed me as it had been redone
around 1890 by some rustic dauber. He had
redressed the characters in the scene like new,
retouched the architecture, introduced textured
draperies into the opening of the windows
through which the Venetian Maremma could
once have been glimpsed. It was enough to
make one cry.

Before descending, I leaned on the railing of
the gallery from where I could, in one glance,

take in the entire ground floor. The central alley was occupied by a catafalque bearing a stretcher on which reposed a nun, left alone provisionally, it seemed, by the sisters who had to watch her. Though dead, this nun, with a belly swollen like a wine skin and a face that seemed to come straight from Daumier's pencil, inspired a deep repulsion in me. She wore the habit of her order, and her sisters had styled her hair with a crown of fat paper roses to signify she was a virgin. Of all the dead I saw, this nun was the only one that inspired neither sympathy nor tenderness: meanness oozed from her entire person. I noted the image with displeasure, but it surprised me into thinking of the frequency with which the necrophiliac meets with the dead, the drunk with the bottle, the gambler with the cards. At the instant I had this reflection, a little man with a long nose and a very devoted air entered the chapel and prostrated himself in front of the altar, making his sign of the cross with the blessed water. Then in the same second that a tremendous clap of thunder resounded

and a torrential rain tried suddenly to penetrate
the chapel, he noticed the stretcher and seemed
electrified. After a brief hesitation, the little
man hurried to the door, which he closed, as he
did the one to the sacristy. Then, protected
from the deluge of all unexpected intrusions, he
looked to the right and to the left to ensure he
was alone, forgetting, nevertheless, to lift his
eyes to the galleries. Reassured, he threw himself
on the Christian, septuagenarian virgin; then,
having taking out a thin, red, bulbous member
resembling that of a Pompeian satyr, he
introduced himself, gasping. Once in, he
worked the nun furiously, who at each of his
thrusts, let out the sharp squeak of a mouse in
heat, all while the crown of paper roses, fallen
into her nose, was jolted about in cadence with
the castanet noise of her rosary. The little fellow
was certainly not an inveterate necrophiliac, at
most he was maybe among those who figure it's
never too late to start. In truth, I think it was
more a case of opportunity making the thief,
and he would have just as well appeased his

✳

brusque needs on a goat. Stamping, jumping, and crying out as if someone had cut off his ears, the little fellow achieved his goal in time to the nun's squeaks and the rolling drum of all the celestial thunder, after which, he readjusted himself with a sheepish look, rearranged the crown of artificial roses, and readjusted the habit of the Lord's spouse before leaving furtively.

I waited a bit longer, and once the storm had moved off, I left in my own turn. The scene had entertained me with its rustic fable flavour, which I saw as a pleasant allegory of the Christian world besieged by paganism. As far as sacrilege, I haven't believed in that for a long time.

January 7, 19...

Sex is spoken of in all its forms except one. Necrophilia isn't tolerated by governments nor approved by questioning youth. Necrophiliac love: the only sort that is pure. Because even *amor intellectualis* — that great white rose — waits to be paid in return. No counterpart for the necrophiliac in love, the gift that he gives of himself awakens no enthusiasm.

From time to time — most often after my nocturnal outings — the local press mobilizes an opinion. They go so far as to come up with ridiculous hypotheses, evoking former medical students searching in the Clamart Cemetery for specimens to dissect or Victorian-era resurrectionists. A particularly spirited hack didn't hesitate to suppurate cannibalistic orgies, something like the amusements of *l'ogre Minski*.

Whatever. It's not sufficient to be as timid as I am; I must also be prudent. I often have the impression that I'm being observed, watched. Especially by service people: cleaning ladies, concierges, neighbourhood merchants. And cops, of course. Especially the cops.

March 15, 19...

Herodotus teaches us that women of quality "after their death are not delivered directly to the embalmers, no more than very beautiful or well-renowned women. They aren't given up

❋

until after three or four days. This is done in order to avoid the embalmers taking advantage of these women."

Scattered in the human chronicle, the most ancient of commentaries on this inoffensive passion that no one calls perversity. But "three or four days" is so naive . . . !

May 10, 19...

Yesterday, one of my clients, a young and charming pianist, tried to seduce me. We were having tea, seated on the little Empire sofa in the library, a piece of furniture that's not very big. I gathered together in mine the two beautiful wandering hands and I gave them back to their owner smiling, as if refusing a pair of birds.

"Oh . . . Lucien. So you're not into boys? I thought that . . ."

"But of course I like boys. And even girls too."

Not able really to say to him, "I would love your eyes sunken in, your lips silenced, your sex frozen, if only you were dead; unfortunately, you have the bad taste to be alive," I hypocritically added, "But I am not single, and I wouldn't want to give occasion for any complications." Too bad.

He believed with much kindness.

June 7, 19...

Hardly a day goes by that I am not reminded of Suzanne, her breasts with their large, beige aureoles, her sunken-in belly suspended like a tent between the two points of her hips, her sex of which the mere memory is sufficient to stir my own. Today, the ivory of her bones, with what marine life has it integrated?

July 1, 19...

The visit from the unmarried woman from Ivry wore me out completely and I only want to sleep alone.

I discovered her tomb by chance as I was going for a stroll in the cemetery to unwind: a completely fresh grave, not even given a name yet. Curious, I asked myself what it might contain and promised to return at night. Now,

the grave contained a pine coffin of inferior
quality — exactly the type that is the most
convenient — in which reclined a woman whom
I brought home without trouble. In all my
loves there is an ineffable moment, the one in
which, for the first time, I discover the face of a
companion whose destiny I am granted, when I
lean avidly over the traits that soon will become
familiar to me.

She must have been between forty and forty-
five, but it's true that death restores youthfulness.
It was a common woman, probably a seamstress,
for her left index finger was hardened and
picked all over with a thousand needle pricks. I
noticed also that the skin on her hands was too
big for the bones: thick as if waterlogged, it was
encircled by a host of heavy folds. This woman
was brown as a Gitane: her eyelids, the points of
her breasts, her sex had this deep, somewhat
violet swarthiness that is found in the velvet of
certain mushrooms or in hydrangeas touched
by frost. Opulent tufts of hair with the lustre of
astrakhan fur dressed her armpits, her pubis.

And above all, she had an extraordinary
moustache: two black commas, thin and supple,
framed her mouth, descending to the bottom
of her cheeks, cruel as those of Genghis Khan.
An original person, no doubt. I couldn't help
but notice, for that matter, that this wasn't the
least of her originalities. She was a virgin, or so
I discovered, in the very second that she ceased
to be. Was she afraid of men or did she hate
them? Had she preferred women? With this
mustache like the lash of a whip . . . With that
extraordinarily virile part of her femininity: a
hard, strong almond overhanging her nymph's
fold . . .

My Ivry virgin had, above all, a confounding
particularity. One might say that in death she
avenged herself of her long abstinence. Never
have I encountered such an unusual sex as
hers, living in this death with a tremendous,
autonomous, unfathomable life. Sometimes it
dilated itself like a fishbowl to the point that I
thought I had lost myself in a sort of abyss, other
times it seized me subtly, held me, fed off me

✳

with a gluttonous lapping. Another disturbing particularity: my sperm disappeared into her without leaving a trace, mysteriously absorbed by this blotter-woman, by this carnivorous plant.

For several days I let myself give in to the temptations of the turbulent Ivry virgin, even if it wasn't without fear, as if, faking death, she would suddenly be able to open her eyes and, reanimated by my substance, devour me. What's more, her agitation grew as the days went on, but, thankfully, the reassuring odour of the bombyx augmented proportionally.

One evening, my mistress suddenly opened her mouth, just as Suzanne had done before. But not having had an education, the Ivry virgin did it with a lion's yawn, revealing at the same time an irregular and badly-cared-for set of teeth. Another time, while avoiding her malicious sex, I searched for passage in her backroad; she omitted a series of incongruities that discouraged me. Without attaching an excessive importance to this type of accident, I prefer from now on that it doesn't repeat itself.

But the Ivry virgin had many pleasant sides, and I am far from forgetting the pleasures she gave me.

Nevertheless, all good things come to an end. Mademoiselle, I thank you for your visit and your company. You are very nice, but all your artifices and your different forms of femininity won't be able to extract from me that which I no longer possess. Absolutely drained, I ask myself if you aren't some sort of succubus. . . .

July 24, 19...

I am strarting to miss my Ivry virgin, my living-dead woman whose palpitating flesh knew how to surround mine and inhale my substance. Something that isn't encountered twice in life, nor twice in death . . . Melancholy over not even knowing her name. Magic that escapes from me. *Nevermore.*

I didn't appreciate that woman enough.

Was I ironic — behaving with the sort of irony that's nothing more than the bad coat of the shameful poor? Did I forget — to forget is to omit from feeling again, it's a folly of the soul and the body — did I then forget that I fall in love each time? One day, by chance, I was walking behind two German students and I heard one say to the other, *"Denn jedesmal, verliebe ich mich heillos . . ."* I could have said the same was true for me. *Ich auch, leider, ich auch . . .* The truth is that I was cowardly enough to blush to myself over the unusual moustached virgin, over my Kirghiz princess with the retractile, recitative vagina. Of course I loved her . . . Unless certain words shouldn't be used, for it seems that the necrophiliac, as he's presented in the twilight of the popular imagination, doesn't have the right to claim them.

Otherwise, a nice episode a few days ago. A *Petit mort pour rire,* around eighteen or twenty years old, alas quite demolished by an accident. But serene, fraternal. A friend I call "Peachskin," even though he had another name and the peach skin in question, far from being his, was merely a vehicular adjuvant.

September 2, 19...

A traumatic, unexpected adventure.

I was going to spend the day in the Fontainebleau forest because the weather was splendid and I had little desire to remain shut up in the store. I stopped at Barbizon for a few minutes. Passing by the bakery, I noticed an announcement: "Closed due to death." My black clothes and my stranger's ways had attracted the attention of an old woman leaning at the window. Without doubt, she thought I had come for the funeral. Actually, she was hardly mistaken; I always come for funerals, for a perpetual mortuary festival, for a wedding funeral. The dead draw me from quite far by unknown labyrinths.

"You arrived too late," said the old lady, "he was interred yesterday afternoon. What a beautiful man! How terrible! The wheel of his delivery truck entered him there."

She indicated the top of her abdomen. I thanked this woman and went on my way. I had read the name on the front of the bakery.

"Pierre," I repeated to myself. Pierre, a beautiful man . . .

I remember the afternoon as if through a fog. I had lost the notion of time, measuring my wait not by my watch but by the light. The light . . . My enemy . . . Why had I been named Lucien, me the lucifuge? Separated from my habitual environment, the hours seemed longer than ever. I slept for a while in the car, and realized with surprise upon waking up that it was already two o'clock in the morning. I would be unable to describe the Barbizon cemetery, certainly banal, with its pearly wreaths and its crying angels. I found the freshest tomb without trouble, surmounted with flowers piled up like hay for a mule. I had no trouble moving the earth, nor in opening the coffin, which, nevertheless, seemed abnormally large.

A beautiful man . . . Heavens! He measured barely less than two metres and was well in proportion. They probably tried to save him at the hospital, for a thick bandage, marked in its centre with a watery stain, squeezed his

✳

monumental torso where the dense brown hair curled. Never had I seen a dead man so calm, with his somewhat heavy Roman profile, his sweet white skin like that flour he kneaded over the years into bread for the living. I had immediately understood that it would be impossible to displace Pierre in a single go. Taking infinite pains, I managed, nevertheless, to extract his body halfway from the coffin. I felt ashamed to enjoy him right on the spot, in the hostility of the open world, with the danger of chance, for the clandestine need walls to protect against terrestrial murmurings, curtains to stop the watchfulness of the stars.

Pierre's head bumped regularly against the wood of the lateral panel; his torso was implicated in the same turning movement that one sees in certain tortured trees, while his waist was folded abruptly over the edge of the coffin, liberating the base, dislocating the long, strong legs. I noticed that Pierre must have often given up in life that which he gave to me in death. That hardly bothered me, but I was saddened by the incongruousness of the posture, the narrowness of the coffin, the sudden charge of a rat. Before leaving Pierre, I laid him out again for better or worse in his coffin and pulled the shroud back over him. He might have passed for a sort of "Christ in the Tomb" in the arms of a profane Joseph of Arimathea.

It was all over the day before yesterday. I feel like it aged me twenty years. That was the first time that I didn't offer one of my funereal friends the comfort of my bed, the calm of my room.

January 12, 19...

"Jerome B., fifteen years. Without occupation. Resident, avenue Henri-Martin. Passy Cemetery. Two p.m."

To be looked into.

January 14, 19...

There were a lot of people at the interment of Jerome, which I attended to be able to find his tomb again more easily. And out of desire,

✳

curiosity, sympathy. Nice, crisp weather. All the upper crust of the sixteenth arrondissement, in cashmere raincoats and mink pelisses. I found myself next to an old lady in a violet hat who never stopped chatting. "Two days of a sickness thought to be benign then wham he had just finished such a good trimester at Janson-de-Sailly the awful grief of his parents poor Charles and especially that poor Zouzou oh, yes for you don't know it maybe but he never called his mother mom but Zouzou those two adored each other in an unimaginable way but are you a part of the family how do you know Jerome?"

I responded that I was his Latin professor, but the old lady carried on immediately with the thread of her monologue.

The parents. Him, very thin, very elegant, lost in his grief as in a faraway country. Her, a young woman with blue eyes tumefied by tears, with an opulent cascade of chestnut hair, poorly concealed by the black veil.

A fat guy, stuffed like a sausage into a fur-lined raincoat approached the tomb and, in an

✳

artificially choked voice, read a funeral prayer
imitating Bossuet. It was the Latin professor.
The real one.

When night arrived, I parked the car near
Pétrarque Square and, once more, all went
without a hitch. It seemed I was protected by
Hermes, god of thieves and guide of the dead.
He inspired a thousand subterfuges in me,
steered the objects of my passion right to my bed
without encumbrance.

Jerome. He is as big as me, but so thin that in
two hands I can almost imprison his hips. He
doesn't know what to do with his long arms, nor
where to place his long legs, more gangling than
a colt's. His chest, his hair, his pointed face have
a salty savour, as if they have been bathed in
tears, but until I had purified it with my saliva
and dried it with my caresses, his sex had the
terrible taste of lavender.

I'm looking at Jerome. I bring him back to
life for a moment of the Infernal Empire. His
private bath opens onto the trees of the avenue.
He is "Pop," because he wanted it that way and

because Zouzou does everything he wants, always a mess with his little flasks that he forgets to cap and his big English soaps all over the place. He even has a useless electric razor, hidden at the bottom of a drawer — no sense in Zouzou noticing it; it would make her laugh. She enters without embarrassment, without even knocking. While he brushes his teeth, he sees her smiling blue eyes in the bathroom mirror. She pinches his butt, ruffles his hair, kisses his neck between the shoulders, there where his vertebrae protrude, then takes off running. He follows her, his mouth full of toothpaste, lashes his towel, which limply slaps the door that she has closed.

Spread out over her bidet, Jerome soaps himself up with lavender, slowly, so slowly. When he closes his eyes, he sees a woman with chestnut hair framing a blank space in which he can't manage to place a face. He forces his imagination, searching for this face with the obstinacy of an insect; suddenly he believes he has found it, but he can't, he can't.

January 15, 19...

Last night, I had moved the armchair in my
room so it faced the large Venetian mirror I
love so much. I had placed Jerome on my lap; I
chewed his neck with its silver sheen, right
between the shoulders, there where Zouzou
surely kissed him in the daytime. In the mirror's
grey fern patterns, among the foliated frost, I
saw Jerome dance like a big marionette
controlled by the movements of my desire.

January 16, 19...

Jerome. Hieronymus. In his *Garden of Earthly
Delights*, Hieronymus Bosch painted two young
men who played with flowers. One of them
planted fond corollas in his companion's anus.

Tonight, I went to look for cypripediums at
the florist, and with them I decorated my friend
Jerome, whose flesh already complements the
subtleties of their orchid-green, brown, and
violet sulphurs. Both have the same plump
brilliance — as if sticky — both achieve that
triumphant state of a substance at its peak — at

the extreme accomplishment of itself — that
precedes effervescence and purification.
Stretched out on his side, Jerome seemed to be
sleeping, his sex introduced into the calyx of a
cypripedium, whose liquor inundated him,
while a cascade of lively flowery odours escaped
from the swarthy bruises that marbleised his
rose-coloured secret.

I had thought that Jerome had his mother's
eyes, but, lifted up, his flaccid eyelid revealed a
deep green, olive-brown iris: the colour that one
finds in the viscous inner walls of cypripediums.

January 20, 19…

Jerome given back to the night, Jerome given
back to the abyss, what currents are you sinking
in, drunken boat?

And me, soon, I will fall into death like
Narcissus into his own image.

April 15, 19…

This morning, I found the apartment invaded
with big blue flies. Where did they come from?

Of course, the cleaning lady was there; she went to look for an insecticide at the druggist's. Horrible. The buzzing bodies were strewn about the carpet, getting smashed all over the place; all the while a chemical odour invaded the apartment, refusing to leave by the windows.

Without letting up, the cleaning lady murmured obscure imprecations that carried menacing allusions: "It's not normal. . . . It was bound to happen. . . . Now that's the last straw. . . . Sure enough, that's what it is. . . . Me, I don't much like this sort of thing. . . ." Etc. Another one who's going to leave me.

April 23, 19...

Found in Tristan Corbière, a very nice expression: "To come like a hanged man."

May 2, 19...

Already it's almost four days since I separated myself from Geneviève and her little one. If I had actually been noticed and identified, as I had feared, I would already have been worried.

Which isn't to say these last hours weren't very trying.

I went to look for the young woman in the Pantin Cemetery, a desolate place. I didn't know what she had died from, so I was surprised to find her with her newborn in her arms. I didn't much appreciate this familial interlude.

Geneviève was truly pretty. She must have suffered a lot, not only in her poor, torn body, but especially in her soul, for her face was imprinted with that particular sadness of those who leave desperate. I loved her transparent colour, her vast pale breasts. Her impassable sex, a horrible thing that I avoided looking at. I turned Geneviève's body around slowly, slipping into the shadow of her superb behind, leaning "like a hanged man" into this strange labyrinth of the snares and misfortunes of the generation.

I played for some time at caressing the baby, a little boy who, nevertheless, was hardly pretty, with his rumpled face, his stunted limbs, his fat head. The icy calmness of his flesh, the odour of bombyx that he emanated very strongly, soon inspired in me more precise games. I placed the baby without a name on my lap, his head reposing on my knees, his legs coming up at a right angle, his feet almost touching my chest. I introduced myself just between his thighs only to soon realize that I wouldn't get any pleasure out of that. His flesh seemed as bland as a cream soup. Stupidly, I persisted anyway, rushing my movements to a conclusion that brought no ecstasy. Someone even stupider than me might have evoked Gilles de Rais, not so much because of the child, but because of the chosen position, conducive to spreading a subject out on his stomach — a subject who, for that matter, wasn't my victim. I don't like Gilles de Rais, a man of a deficient sexuality, eternal little boy who never stopped committing suicide through others. Gilles de Rais disgusts me. There's only one dirty thing: the suffering one can cause. I didn't keep Geneviève and her baby very long, but the story had a follow-up, or at least, with a bit of bad luck, could easily have had one.

I cast off the bag into which I had placed the

two of them, held in each other's arms, so that
nothing could separate them before their bones
fled into the currents, becoming porous and
light like pieces of pumice stone, crumbling and
disappearing to be reunited in the lime of
starfish. At the very instant when the water
closed over them, doors banged into the silence
of the night, cries resounded. On the bank,
men ran in my direction. "Hey there! Hey!" —
"Over there! Over there!" No doubt, I had been
seen by the gas factory workers. They chased me
like dogs chasing a hare and, like the hare, I ran,
zigzagging, to cross the nocturnal streets of
Leval. Sometimes their clamour approached
dangerously, but all of a sudden they seemed to
lose all trace of me. I heard them call each
other, shout out injunctions, advice. The walls
covered in lacerated posters, the blind facades of
warehouses, the abandoned factories passed by at
my sides with a dreamlike rhythm. Not knowing
where I was, running lost into the maze of
hostile streets, I feared, above all, to trap myself
in a dead end. And suddenly, the miracle I

hadn't counted on: my good old Chevrolet, carriage for all my marriages, wisely stationed along the sidewalk. While I was starting up, I had enough time to perceive, along the edge of a wall, a group of men gesticulating wildly in the light from a streetlamp. *Once more saved!*

June 15, 19...

It's already more than a month that I've been in Naples, very happy to be far away from Paris for a while. I confided my business to a manager who had already taken good care of it four years ago when I stayed in Nice. To tell the truth, the nocturnal chase in Leval greatly affected me. I smelled danger. Not to mention I really wanted to rediscover Naples, the most macabre of cities. Naples, the mouth of Hades. The dead are played with there like big dolls. They are embalmed, inhumed, exhumed, cleaned, decorated, coiffed; they get their sockets stuffed with green or red bulbs, placed in recesses on a wall, get dressed standing up in glass coffins. They get dressed, they get undressed, and nothing is

✳

more bizarre than those stiff mummies in their
tight clothes, coiffed in tow wigs, a bouquet of
dusty wax flowers in their hands. At San
Domenico Maggiore, the queens of Aragon,
monkey-women in brown leather, shrivelled up
in their coffins. The sacristan lifts the coffin lid
with one hand, extending the other for his tip
— Hermes is also Mercury. But all these
mummies are too dried out to please or
illuminate the senses much. They lack internal
movement and fresh metamorphoses.

Naples . . . Less than a hundred years ago,
they still paraded cadavers through the streets
like in ancient Rome. Today, one encounters
nothing but massive death carriages, flanked by
gigantic lanterns, decorated with black ostrich
feathers.

July 2, 19...

Intermezzo all'improvviso . . . I came back from
visiting the Santa Chiara cloister and, wanting
to descend towards the Corso Umberto, I took
this fantastic staircase described by Malaparte:

the Pendino Santa Barbara, where only female dwarves live. Horrible, deformed, often bald, sometimes holding children in their arms who seemed to be made out of grey rags, the dwarves lived there in a restless yelping. Big cavernicolous insects, they occupy the *bassi*, those rooms without windows that open onto the street at foot level, each of them identical: a large bed covered in pink nylon, a television set, and pious imagery.

In front of one of the *bassi*, a crowd of dwarves obstructed the stairs, chattering in a plaintive tone, while those who seemed the most affected occupied the obscure cave where the lamps glowed brightly as if it were the middle of the night. Death had come by there and my heart made that old leap that I knew well. What's more, the dwarves hurried to inform me that one of them, their good friend, Teresa, had just been lifted up to the Heavens. I offered to join them in honouring Teresa at her wake. They accepted with an excitation that was indescribable even for Naples.

Teresa's crumpled, ashen face could have been thirty years old just as well as seventy-five, crowned by indefinable clumps in the guise of hair. She'd been put into a sort of first communion dress that came up to her ears, for she was humpbacked. Several of her companions, climbing on the bed, worked at pawing her, patting her, kissing her, lifting a lock of her impossible hair, caressing her cheek, smoothing out a fold in her dress — all with the monstrous cackling of an aviary. I learned that Teresa had been run over by a car while crossing the via Sedile di Porto and that, with two severed thighs, she lost all her blood before getting sufficient help. It's true that a dwarf can't have very much blood. Lots of gestures were made, lots of cries were let out, and lots of advice was given, but Teresa was already out of blood when the ambulance arrived.

She was brought back to her house; her friends washed, combed, and protected her. She was redressed in white, a sign, they said, that Teresa died a virgin. Virgin or not, I

swear that she awakened my desire much more
actively than it has been for a long time already,
I haven't . . .

Happily, as the weather was still stormy, I was
armed with a raincoat that I carried on my arm
and thanks to which it was possible for me to
cover the state I was in. I only asked myself how
I was going to take Teresa out of a district this
populated without the help of a car. I forged a
thousand plans, one more absurd than the next,
as I listened to the chattering dwarves. The heat
was stifling. Noon approached. The voices
started dragging as they thickened in the vitreous
air. The odour of something fried rose to the
mortuary bed and the dwarves couldn't help but
notice it. There was a sort of wavering or a lull
in their lamentations. One of them spoke of
making coffee. I intervened, offering them a
funeral lunch in the neighbouring restaurant, as
long as they could excuse their host for not
taking part himself: he would take over the death
watch so that they could all eat together.
Enchanted, they accepted the invitation and a

✳

quarter of an hour later, when I returned to the
restaurant where I had prepared their feast, I
found them already draped in black satin shawls,
coiffed in peculiar antique hats flowered with
crepe irises. They welcomed me with cries of joy,
then scattered themselves around the Pendino
like a flock of crows.

I was alone with Teresa. I closed the door,
and, slowly, calmly, undid my tie.

July 16, 19...

I just visited Capodimonte, the park of mossy
tritons with the long yellow château that shelters
a marvellous collection of paintings behind the
bouquets of palm trees. *La morte de Pétrone* by
Pacecco de Rosa . . . An animated composition,
but one from which indifference transpires:
beautiful, limpid colours, but no intuition of
the subject. At least not mine.

Even here, in Naples, in the calm of his villa,
Caius Petronius Arbiter, a grand lord, a grand
poet, a compromised man, had his veins opened
by his doctor. Surrounded by his concubines

and his Greek slaves slipping their tongues into
his mouth and caressing his hair, which had
been mussed by the bath steam, he saw their gaze
erased from behind a veil because his own gaze
was being snuffed out like a lamp. He heard
their tender words pull back towards another
planet because he himself was about to leave the
earth. Supported by their arms, no doubt, he
still had time to measure his solitude. Bowled
over by the sweetness of their smiles, he sensed
their hands close upon his already inert
member; the only force that gushed from him
came together into a vermillion coral twig, the
perfect arc of which united his wrist with the
silver basin. He sensed nothingness invade the
network of his veins, the night penetrate his
flesh, from his pierced earlobes to his long
phalanxes folded under the weight of his rings,
while the dancers stuck their vulvas to his body
like barnacles onto a ship and the fingers of
these ephebi explored his secret parts. Floating
into his bath as if into the maternal liquid,

Caius Petronius Arbiter sensed his life escaping
him as sweetly as it had once come to him.

That's how death should be.

August 5, 19...

The San Gaudioso catacombs. Those in Paris
are nothing in comparison; one must go to
Naples to see something like that. Baroque,
fantastic, the San Gaudioso catacombs spread
out over an immense distance and it is even said
that certain forgotten galleries join those of San
Gennaro. Women come here to implore the
favours of the "souls of Purgatory," as they
naively call the infernal forces, and to practise
the worship of bones.

The skulls, often polished with wax, coiffed
with wigs, and set on little private altars by the
faithful, who are, for that matter, total strangers
to them, make for the object of a very active
trade on the guardians' part. The atmosphere of
these pagan catacombs — for that's exactly what
they are — is absolutely unreal. The murmured
prayers, the shadows of women projected by the

flickering candles onto the macabre, rocky
stones, the skeletons and the clothed mummies
in their niches, the odour of bones and of
offerings form an indescribable environment.
Straight off, I was enthusiastic.

Finding myself in a less frequented gallery,
my attention was suddenly solicited by the little
games of one of the faithful. It was a fat little
woman like they all are over there. She must
have been around thirty years old and visibly
belonged to the middle class; maybe she was the
wife of a local merchant or a subordinate official.
With one knee resting on the seat of a chair, she
leaned over its back, her rump jutting out and
her neck held forward, bringing her face closer
until she touched a skull set on the molding.
The profile of the woman and that of the skull
detached themselves neatly in the reddish glare
of a lamp, the one cupped under the smile of
the other. The woman had succeeded in
introducing her tongue into the jaw, and, lit
from behind, I saw it lick and wriggle between
the dead teeth, bent and pointed like a horn of

✳

coral — that old phallic symbol the Neapolitans
wear against the evil eye.

At times, the woman brought that tongue,
which I guessed would be surprisingly hard and
fleshy, up to the incisors of the dead, running
it along the exterior of the teeth like a hand
caressing a keyboard; at other times, she
plunged it in as far as she could to lick the inside
of the molars and the roof of the mouth.

She was enjoying herself so much that she
hadn't heard me approach. I observed her for a
while before she suddenly noticed my presence
and sat up, stifling a cry.

"You have nothing to fear from me," I told
her, "but don't you want to get back to what you
were doing just now?"

The woman studied me with distrust. I
repeated my request, and the flash of an idea
that no doubt seemed brilliant to her spread
across her face:

"If someone sees me, I will say that it's you
that forced me to do it."

I confess that I was confounded by this vulgar

ruse with which she managed to turn around the situation. But already, and without saying another word, she had returned to her skull, the eyes half-closed, the tongue stuck out.

That which was unusual about the spectacle and the place, combined with the euphoria I felt as soon as I had entered the catacombs, had an effect on me that a necrophiliac doesn't often experience. I wanted this woman, even though she was alive. I lifted up her black dress and, pulling down her cotton underwear, I discovered a large rump, polished and diaphanous as the wax of the candles around us. It was even smoother to the touch than the sight. Having slipped my hand into the crack, I pulled out my fingers soaked in an opaline liquor that disconcerted me — the dead don't secrete anything like that — and would have repulsed me if its odour hadn't recalled that of the sea, image and sister of the dead. And so, the thought that all flesh carries within itself the seed of its destruction revived the desire I had for this woman, but that desire abandoned me the very

✳

instant I tried to make deeper contact, like a house of cards that collapses as soon as it is touched. The woman turned towards me, her face distorted with anger:

"I'm going to say that you tried to get violent with me."

I didn't understand why her resentment led her to threaten me like that. In any case, I distanced myself as quickly as I could.

In my apartment in Posillipo, I felt suddenly invaded with bitterness and sadness. I wanted to live and I wanted to die, but I couldn't live nor die. Is that the Garden of Gethsemane?

September 12, 19…

I don't know why, but this morning while fixing my tie, I briefly recalled a very old image of my neighbour from adolescence, that Gabrielle who pleased me so much when she appeared to me hanged, the eyes sunken back in her head in a last ecstasy.

October 16, 19...

I am tempted to believe that Hecate has cast a benevolent regard over me. Death is kind to me, the tireless purveyor of my pleasures — and if they are sometimes incomplete, it's only due to my own debility.

A long time ago, I might have thought of the happiness that the simultaneous presence of two bodies would bring me, and I might have imagined in my mind's eye a sort of tableau vivant (or more like a still life). Something, in any case, that I never really counted on, a forgotten dream, returned to the night where dreams dissolve.

I was very stupid to not believe in miracles.

Tonight, I want to record every detail of the adventure so that I can remember them all, for everything is happening so quickly and in such an unexpected way that I feel like my memory is threatened. It's true that I always feel, in some way, as if a part of myself, if not my whole being, is under some obscure threat. Or under the threat of a threat.

I went to Sorrento and, on the way back, I stopped for a glass of wine at Vico Equense, in a hotel where they know me. Built into the edge of a cliff, the hotel dominates a little cove closed off by rocks, which is accessed by an elevator, the interior of which is always dripping. As it was the middle of the week, with the season already over even if the sea was still warm, the hotel and its beach were empty. A deserted feeling weighed on the terraces, the bar, the dining room. It was like a veil, a detention, a constraint. In the hall, I bumped into the patron and remarked that he really looked out of it. The staff whispered to each other. When Giovanni, the one who serves me the most often, brought my wine, I asked him why everyone seemed so troubled. He looked around carefully to the left and right before confiding in me in a half-whisper:

"It's because of the two Swedes, the brother and sister, two young clients who were fished out of the water this morning. Those two who swam like fish! One of them must have had some trouble and the other wanted to help. Yep . . .

drowned, it really gets you . . . as if they did it on purpose to not die alone. . . . But what a blow for the hotel!"

He also taught me that the two swimmers had been fished out right after the accident, though there had been no success in reviving them, and that the first steps had been taken in Naples to have the Swedish Consulate warn the parents — they were surely going to arrive by plane, concluded Giovanni — and that the two drowned bodies might even be transported to their own country to be buried. Until then, the bodies had been left in the little grotto on the beach since no one came there in the off-season and the beach huts had already been taken down. It seemed that all my blood went straight to my heart. I put a mask of indifference over my face and pretended to interest myself with other things. Is it possible? I repeated to myself. How? I had to come up with a seamless plan. In less than an hour, it was developed. I left the hotel and took the drivable road that leads to the Faito summit to wait for night. I couldn't truly hide from myself that the mission was full of danger. My entire project could degenerate into a horrible catastrophe at an unexpected interruption: the sudden barking of a dog, an encounter with octopus fishers who sought their booty almost every night with enormous lamps. . . . But I was determined. It was simply a question of acting calmly and quickly. Nervous, edgy, extremely emotive in daily life, I have a tremendous reserve of calmness and aptness as soon as it's a question of carrying off a dead body. I become another person. I'm suddenly a stranger to myself, all the while being more myself than ever. I stop being vulnerable. I stop being unhappy. I reach a sort of quintessence of myself; I fill the task that fate has destined for me.

Around six o'clock, the rain started falling with enough force to send away the threat of the fishers with their *lampare*. I experienced a happy urgency. Two hours later, I took the road to Seiano, where the landing is more convenient than the one at Vico. I left the car in the bus garage, a murky, rusted hanger with an oil-spotted floor, which is never closed because its door no longer closes.

Today there are only a few rickety houses, just two or three hundred years old, there where once stood the villa of Seianus. All the lights were out except the lamppost at the edge of the pier that blinks each night with a false glow. There was the sound of crackling rain and the sea's undertow between the rocks. I headed toward a boat I had spotted that afternoon, a nasty old plank-board shell that I detached without noise. I rowed to the hotel beach. There, too, the lights were out. Unable to land on the pebbly shore, I took off my pants, attached the boat to a rocky protrusion, and, entering the water up to my thighs, I advanced toward the grotto. The night, the whispering rain, the voice of the sea, and above all the thought of what I was going to discover intoxicated me. I lifted up the cover that concealed the two bodies and carried them one at a time into the boat. Then I went back to Seiano, rowing as quickly as I could. I didn't yet have the time to appreciate the sight of

✳

my dead ones, but they seemed as light as
children. Once again, everything went without a
hitch, even though I had to execute each
manoeuvre twice. I carried the Swedes into the
car, where I had some difficulty getting them in.
They were already stiff, but I managed to arrange
them diagonally on the backseat, the one against
the other, hidden with a cover.

I don't deny that going up in the elevator to
my apartment was one of the most critical
moments of the whole undertaking. I had the
same problem, for that matter, in Paris, and I'd
often thought of renting or buying a ground level
apartment more favourable to my love affairs.

When I had laid out the Swedish adolescents
on my bed, I didn't regret my trouble. They
must have been sixteen or seventeen years old
and I have never seen anything as beautiful as
those two. They resembled each other in an
indescribable way and had no doubt been twins.
Death had changed the quality of their tans,
which the salt had frosted into a gold of a
strange, subtle pallor comparable to that given

✳

off by a candle flame. Each of them had a long
asexual body — the virility of the boy hardly
stood out; the breasts of the girl were practically
nonexistent, though infinitely desirable, and
evoked I don't know which angelic nature to my
eyes. The languor of their silvery-blond hair,
the absence of eyebrows above their severely
bulging eyelids, their protruding cheekbones —
like those of fleshless skulls — and the evanescent
colour of their thin, mauve lips, expressed in
them a most mortal predestination. Strangers to
the world of the living, they had been made to
die and, right from the start, Death had
passionately marked them.

Now that they are in my presence, I hardly
dare approach their beauty.

Outside, the tempest has let up and shakes
the trees of Posillipo. Enormous clouds roll
across the sky. Hecate's dogs roar past.

October 17, 19...

I'm acting as I did for Suzanne, sending away
the staff, forbidding any disturbance, turning

off the heat, establishing cold drafts. Certainly,
I am far from feeling for my beautiful angels the
tender fraternity, the love that united me to
Suzanne, but their splendour moves me and I
want to keep them a long time.

October 18, 19...

I put them to bed in the arms of one another,
interlacing them tenderly, placing the lips of the
brother against those of the sister, putting the
sleeping sex of the one between the delicate
nymphs of the other, at the entrance to that
crack with a pallor and tightness that reminded
me of the one belonging to the little octopus
girl, the one who vomited black juice. I wanted
their bodies, which so often in life had to call to
each other in secret, to be united finally in
death. For I know that these two loved each other
as the sky loves the earth. And the one wanted to
save the other and the other took the one along.
Brought along by love, into the depths, into the
salt and the seaweed, into the foam and the
sands, into the icy sea currents that are stirred

up by the stare of the moon and become as agitated as semen. It wasn't with me that they celebrated their sublime honeymoon, but at the precise instant when the one clung on to the other, the two had exhaled their life at the same time in a shared rapture, united in the water as they were once united in the maternal liquid, in the mother sea as in their own mother, discovering themselves again in their end as they had been confused at their beginning. They had reached their cosmic truth, foreign to the lying world of the living. I contemplated them a long time, recognizing in the spectacle a sort of grace. Not for a moment did I dream of interfering with them, troubling their union with the impure contact of my living flesh.

October 20, 19...

My chaste resolutions abandoned me yesterday evening for a moment, I confess. I was seated near them on the bed, and just for fun, I nibbled the neck of the boy — or was it the girl? — at the precise spot where it comes from the

base of the skull, the round container of which I
could feel on my upper lip. My mouth started a
delicious journey on its own, lightly mounting
and descending along the vertebrae as if
exploring a varied landscape in which the
slightest protrusions integrate themselves into
the vastest undulations of plains and mountains.
I went from dorsal desert to that lumbar valley,
full of feeling and tenderness — a place that
always infinitely moves me — before progressing
into the little arid plateau that lies in front of
the ravine of delights. My hands followed the
journey of my tongue, forming a nonchalant
rearguard. During this whole tour, my sex was
inert; this was nothing for me but a chaste
caress. But when my fingers reached that valley
dug out behind the waist and my nails brushed
against that precise vertebra that was secretly
robust for having, through osmosis, absorbed
the aggression of belts, the desire washed over
me with such violence that I was completely lost.
Beside myself, I passed my head quickly under a
thigh — was it the girl's or the boy's? — and stuck

my mouth to the angelic point where their sexes touched. Their sexes: two infant mollusks, quite soft, flaccid, and covered with that pinkish hue that appears on the skin of the dead when the flesh is going to start changing. My excitation had put me into a sort of delirium, and I'd hardly started passionately licking the point of encounter where these beautiful dead creatures united my desire, when I thought I would die myself and inundated myself, moaning. And unexpectedly, for that matter, for it had been months since I'd managed any sort of ecstasy.

October 22, 19...

My angels radiate a rainbow. How beautiful they are. Their union: *Trionfo délia Morte* . . .

October 28, 19...

From time to time, I correct their position, for my beautiful dead ones with the white nails are deteriorating. They opened their sad shadowy mouths; their necks are folded like stems touched by frost. Their violet and green skin . . . Their members are getting lopsided.

It has been a long time since I forgot the dry odour of the bombyx, and now it's that smell of decay that invades the air. A flask of that black juice that the octopus child vomited spreads over the bellies of the angels, a putrid ink that goes through the mattress, drips on the floor, a pestilential sap that intoxicates me like that of the mandrake. This liquor came slowly from them, though it's water from a very ancient source; it chortles with an embarrassed voice from the edges of their intestines, leaps up, and pours out. Their eyes fall back into the inside of their skulls, as those of the delicious old Marie-Jeanne once did. In them, I think I have found all my dead ones again, even if none of them that I loved ever got to such an advanced state. Not even little Henri.

October 30, 19...

That's already the third time that someone has rung my bell and knocked furiously at my door. Bad sign. The concierge calls me: "Don

❋

Luciano! Don Luciano!" I hear whispers, discussions, muffled exclamations, footsteps.

I don't want to go out. I haven't eaten anything since yesterday, but that doesn't matter. I have some whisky left and tap water, awfully chlorinated, true. Sometimes I have the impression that my angels get up and walk around the apartment, making sure that I don't notice them.

October 31, 19...

Someone just slipped something under my door. I distinctly perceived the miniscule rustling. Under the door to my room, I can already make out a pale, flat spot on the somber marble of the vestibule; it threatens me, though it's only half visible on the threshold, an arrow that links my universe back to that of the living.

I advance slowly, bend over, and pull, hoping to see it dissolve in a cloud of steam like a bad fantasy. No. A message. I won't read it in the room, temple of the Dead, nor in the salon, but in the work area, the bathroom, or the kitchen.

※

Yes, the kitchen. In opening the letter, I already know what it contains. "Convocation de la Questure" — that's what they call the judiciary police here — "for an affair concerning you . . ." That could easily pass for an international jargon of low Esperanto. "For an affair concerning you . . ."

I place the paper on the kitchen table, slowly, very slowly, and the very moment the yellowish form — covered with official stamps and fingerprints — touches the plastic surface, I know that, truly, there is only one, sole affair that still concerns me.

An affair concerns me . . .

I look at my watch. In a few hours it will be November.

November, which always brings me something unexpected, though it has always been prepared. . . .